Stories of fairies

Anna Lester

Illustrated by Teri Gower

Reading Consultant: Alison Kelly
Roehampton University

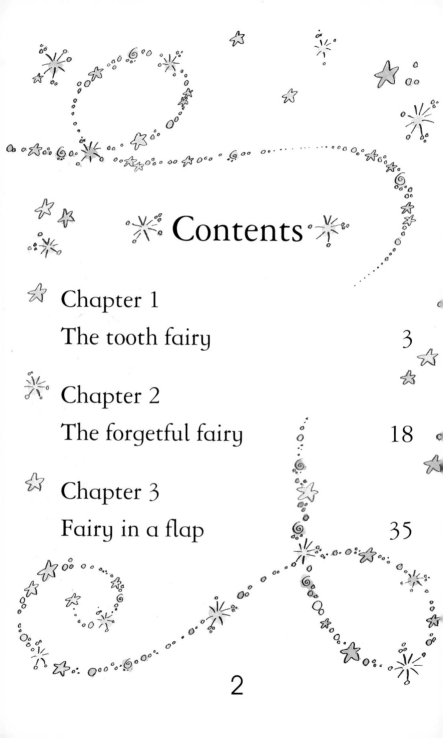

Contents

Chapter 1

The tooth fairy

It was a fantastic day for Crystal. She had passed her final test at the tooth fairy training school.

Now she could turn children's baby teeth into money.

Jet, Crystal's lazy classmate, had failed all her tests. She would never be a tooth fairy.

It's not fair!

As Jet grumbled, the others flew home and prepared for their first trips.

4

That night, Crystal checked that she had everything she needed...

Check!

one bag of magic travel dust...

Check!

one list of children to visit...

Check!

and, most importantly, her wand.

Crystal sprinkled herself with magic dust. The next second, she was in the bedroom of her first customer, Beth Bingly.

Crystal flew up to the bed. Carefully, she lifted a tooth out from under Beth's pillow.

She aimed her wand at Beth's tooth. "*Zapanasha*!" she cried. But instead of a shiny, new coin, she saw...

A ham sandwich?

A hamster?

A cactus?

Every time she aimed her wand, the tooth changed into something – but never a coin.

7

Crystal burst into tears. "It's all gone wrong," she sobbed.

Her crying woke Beth, who couldn't believe her eyes.

"Are you the tooth fairy?" she whispered in amazement.

"Yes," wept Crystal, "but it's my first night and I'm useless."

Crystal explained how her wand had failed. "Everyone in Fairyland will laugh at me," she sobbed. "What can I do?"

Beth felt sorry for the fairy. "Let me go back with you," she said. "Maybe I can help."

"Thank you," Crystal sniffed.

A sprinkle of travel dust later, Beth was in Fairyland. The magic powder had made her fairy-sized. She could fly too!

Beth gasped as she entered the shop. The walls were lined with hundreds of fairy outfits.

There were sparkly tiaras, silky bows, shiny shoes and pots and pots of gleaming wands.

"How can I help you?" asked the shopkeeper.

Crystal explained and the
shopkeeper examined the wand.
"This is Jet's wand," she said.
"It will never work properly,
because she's such a bad fairy."

"That sneaky fairy has
swapped her wand for mine,"
cried Crystal.
"Let's get it back," said Beth.

Jet was lazing on the terrace of her tree house. She'd used Crystal's wand to magic up a huge pile of cream cakes.

This is the life.

She was just about to gulp down her tenth eclair, when Crystal and Beth arrived.

"Hand over my wand, you thief!" demanded Crystal.

13

"No way, Miss Perfect," said Jet. A stream of stars shot from the wand in her hand. The magical blast turned Crystal's feet to stone.

Can't catch me!

Jet raised the wand to strike again. But suddenly it was snatched from her grasp.

"I'll take that," cried Beth, from a branch above Jet's head.

14

Jet tried to fly up and grab the wand back. But she'd eaten so much, she couldn't get off the ground.

Grrr! Give it back!

A second blast from the wand lifted the stony spell from Crystal's feet. She fluttered up to join Beth. "So long, Jet!" cried Crystal as they flew away.

The pair returned to the Fantastic Fairy Store. Crystal bought Beth her very own fairy outfit to thank her.

Then Beth joined the fairies for a midnight feast and they danced until dawn.

"Time to say goodbye," said Crystal, showering Beth in magic dust.

In a flash, Beth was back in bed. "What an amazing dream," she thought.

Beth peeked under her pillow. She expected to see her tooth, or even a coin. But what she saw was the tiniest dress in the world.

17

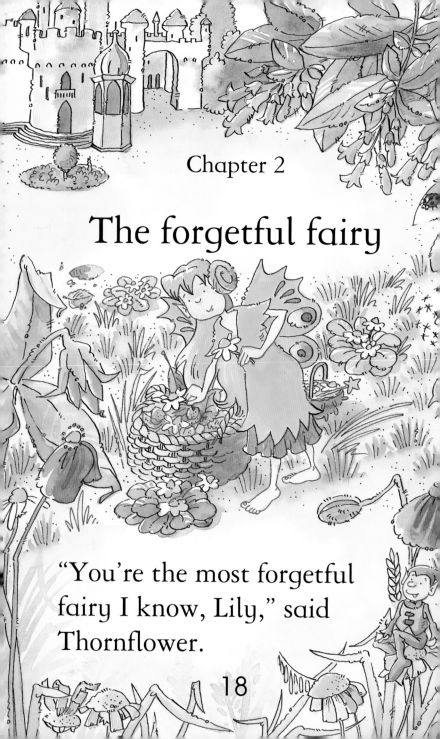

Chapter 2

The forgetful fairy

"You're the most forgetful
fairy I know, Lily," said
Thornflower.

"Since the Fairy Queen's been away, you haven't watered the flowers *or* watched the gnomes. Look at the mess they've made."

"It's time *I* became the Fairy Palace Manager."

"I'm going to make it up to the Fairy Queen," said Lily. "I'm going to organize the best Fairy Ball *ever*."

"Let's hope so," said the Fairy Queen, coming up behind them.

Lily worked
hard all week.
She organized the
Fairy Band.

Bzzzz

Bzzzz

Bzzzz

"Well done, Lily," said the Fairy Queen.

Thornflower was furious. "At this rate, I'll never get her job," she thought angrily.

"Here are the invitations," the Fairy Queen added. "Don't forget, *anyone* with an invitation can come, so only give them to guests on the list."

Lily put the invitations in her
basket and Thornflower's face
lit up in a huge smile.

The hole's still
there!

Lily flew all over Fairyland.
She visited the Rainbow
Fairies and the Garden Fairies.

She even flew over the Wild Woods, to reach the elves and pixies by the Sunset Sea.

It was only when
Lily got home that
she saw the hole in
her basket.

"Oh no!" she sobbed.
"I forgot to patch it
up. Some of the
invitations might
have dropped out...
and *anyone* could
have found one!"

On the night of the Fairy Ball, Lily stood nervously by the Fairy Queen, watching her welcome each of the guests.

"Well done, Lily," said the Queen. "For once, I don't think you've forgotten a thing."

Just then, the ground began to shake.

"What can that be?" said the Fairy Queen. Then she gasped.

An enormous, evil-looking troll was walking up the hill to the Fairy Palace.

Lily turned white.

"Don't worry," said the Fairy Queen. "I've cast a spell. Only guests with invitations can come into the palace tonight."

"The trouble is..." Lily began, "I think that troll might *have* an invitation."

30

He did. There was a loud crash and the troll stuck his huge, green head straight through the palace door.

"Help!" cried the Fairy Queen. "He'll eat us alive."

"This is all your fault, Lily," said Thornflower, gleefully.

31

But the next moment, there was a loud bang followed by a horrible smell. The troll had vanished. In his place stood a Fairy Prince.

"At last!" he cried. "A wicked fairy turned me into a troll. Only coming to a fairy ball could set me free."

"When I found an invitation in the Wild Woods, I was overjoyed."

"I'm so sorry," Lily said to the Fairy Queen. "It was that hole in my basket..."

The Fairy Queen looked thoughtful.

"Never mind, Lily," she said. "The Ball is perfect. And," she added, "it's not every fairy who can turn a troll into a prince."

Chapter 3

Fairy in a flap

Poppy was almost a perfect fairy. Her wand twinkled, her wings shone and her spells never went wrong.

But Poppy
had a problem...

...she couldn't fly.

At school, her friends soared into the sky. Poppy couldn't get off the ground.

"Just keep trying," said the teacher. Poppy flapped her wings until they hurt, but she didn't even hover.

Her mother took her to the
fairy doctor.

"Hmm..." he said. "Stretch
out like a butterfly."

Poppy's wings fluttered open.

And flap...

"She seems fine," he said,
"but try this potion." And he
mixed honey with fluffy clouds.

The potion was delicious, but it didn't help Poppy fly.

"How do you do it?" she asked her best friend, Daisy.

Daisy shrugged. "It just happens," she said.

While her friends did aerobatics, Poppy was stuck in the baby class. As she flapped her wings, a tear rolled down her cheek.

Just then, an imp went past. "What a big baby," he jeered.

Poppy ran from the class sobbing. She didn't stop until she reached the forest. Still crying, she hid in a hollow tree.

"Whooo's that?" hooted an owl grumpily. "Why the fuss?"

41

Hiccuping, Poppy told him.
"Imps are so rude," tutted
the owl. "As for learning to fly,
I can teach you. I've taught
hundreds of fledglings."

42

"Jump off a low branch," he ordered, "and flap your wings."

Concentrating hard, Poppy jumped, flapped... and dropped straight to the ground.

"Oooh dear," the owl hooted. "You're thinking about it too much. Never mind. We'll try again tomorrow."

Back at home, Poppy was making a bandage from blackberry leaves when Daisy burst in.

I've found a spell to make you fly!

44

Before Poppy could stop her,
Daisy had waved her wand
and gabbled a spell.

Leave the ground and touch the sky...
Voll-ah-ray Poppy you will fly!

"I feel the same," Poppy said,
doubtfully.

"Try it!" urged Daisy,
pushing her through the door.
"I won't watch."

Poppy took a deep breath
and opened her wings.
Suddenly, she heard a cry.
One of the baby fairies
was stuck high up
in a sunflower.
    "Hold on!"
she called and
flew up to the
frightened baby.

As she fluttered back down,
Daisy raced out. "Poppy,
wait. I got the spell wrong..."
She stopped. "Poppy?"

"Yes," said Poppy, with a
big grin. "I can fly!"

With thanks to Russell Punter,
Susanna Davidson and Lesley Sims

Designed by Louise Flutter

First published in 2006 by Usborne Publishing Ltd., Usborne House,
83-85 Saffron Hill, London EC1N 8RT, England. www.usborne.com
Copyright © 2006 Usborne Publishing Ltd.